Bob and the Bandstand

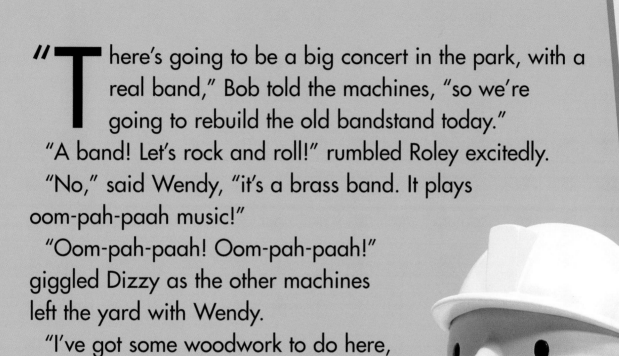

"There's going to be a big concert in the park, with a real band," Bob told the machines, "so we're going to rebuild the old bandstand today."

"A band! Let's rock and roll!" rumbled Roley excitedly.

"No," said Wendy, "it's a brass band. It plays oom-pah-paah music!"

"Oom-pah-paah! Oom-pah-paah!" giggled Dizzy as the other machines left the yard with Wendy.

"I've got some woodwork to do here, first," Bob called as he waved goodbye.

3

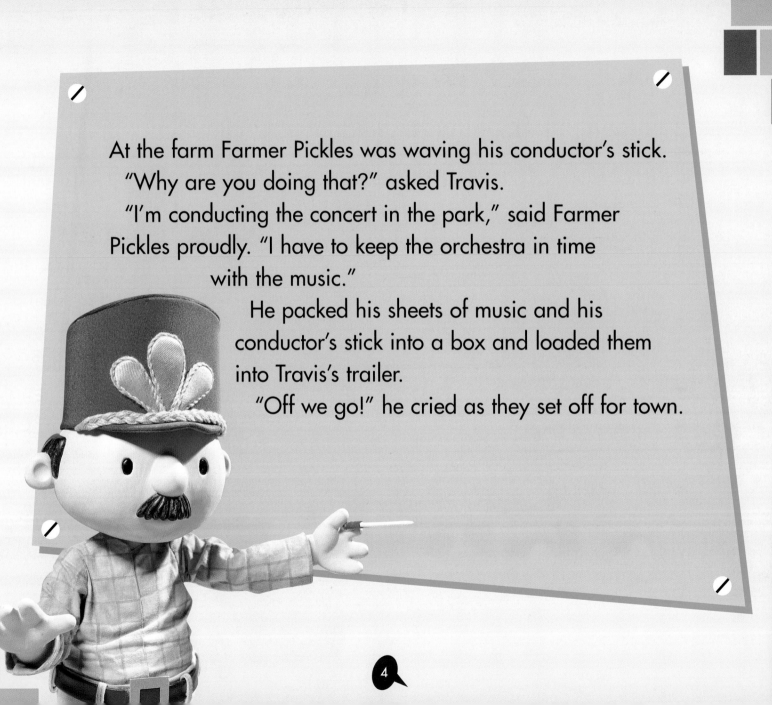

At the farm Farmer Pickles was waving his conductor's stick.
"Why are you doing that?" asked Travis.
"I'm conducting the concert in the park," said Farmer Pickles proudly. "I have to keep the orchestra in time with the music."

He packed his sheets of music and his conductor's stick into a box and loaded them into Travis's trailer.

"Off we go!" he cried as they set off for town.

On their way into town they passed Spud.

"Where are you going?" he asked.

"My band's playing in the park," said Farmer Pickles.

"Ooh, I love playing in the park!" Spud called after them. But Travis and Farmer Pickles were already trundling down the bumpy road.

Suddenly Travis's wheel hit a stone, and with a bump, Farmer Pickles's box of sheet music fell out of the trailer and onto the road!

When Wendy got to the old bandstand, Mr Bentley, the building inspector, was waiting for her.

"The new bandstand will be ready for the grand opening, won't it?" Mr Bentley asked anxiously.

"Of course it will," said Wendy. "Leave it to us, Mr Bentley!"

Meanwhile, Spud had found Farmer Pickles's box of music and conductor's stick.

"Hmmm, I can use this old stick for scaring the crows," he said.

Then he saw the sheets of music, "Ah ha!" he cried, and folded them up to make paper planes.

"Look out, crows!" yelled Spud as he whizzed the planes into the air. He hit one crow right on the beak!

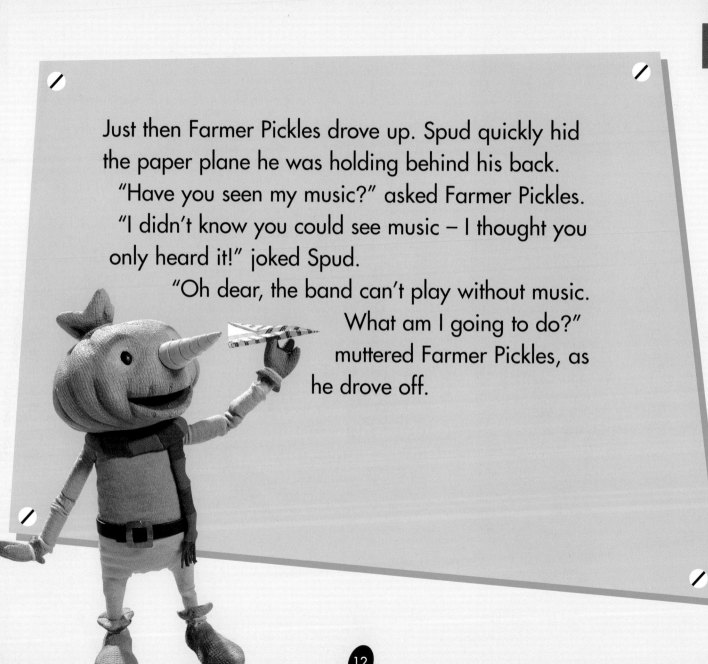

Just then Farmer Pickles drove up. Spud quickly hid
the paper plane he was holding behind his back.

"Have you seen my music?" asked Farmer Pickles.

"I didn't know you could see music – I thought you
only heard it!" joked Spud.

"Oh dear, the band can't play without music.
What am I going to do?"
muttered Farmer Pickles, as
he drove off.

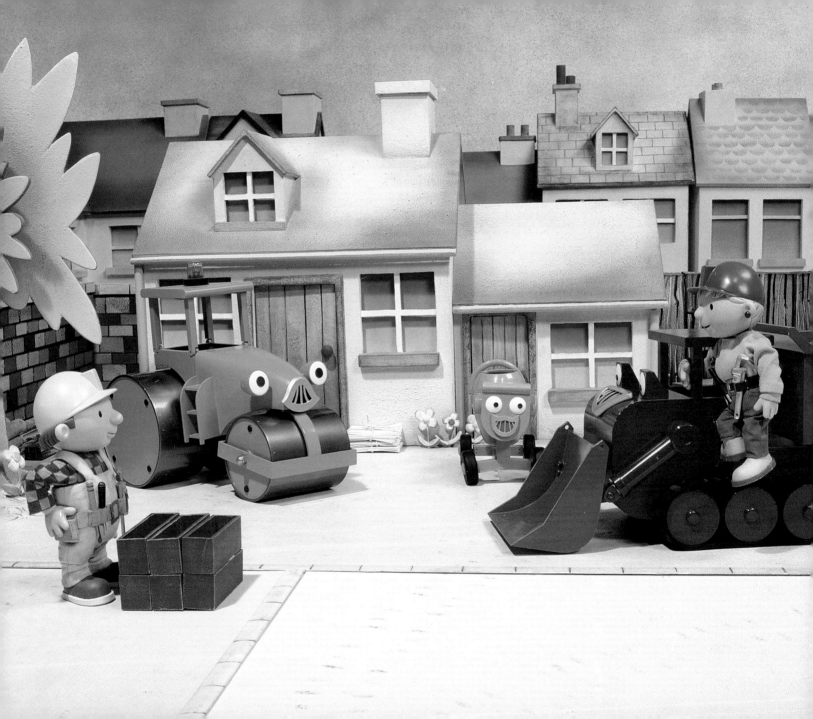

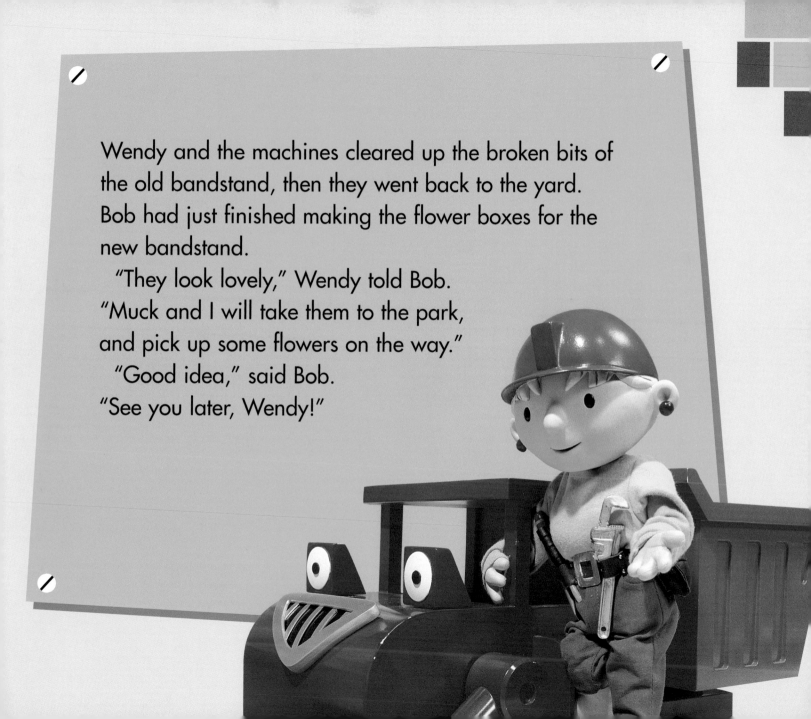

Wendy and the machines cleared up the broken bits of the old bandstand, then they went back to the yard. Bob had just finished making the flower boxes for the new bandstand.

"They look lovely," Wendy told Bob.
"Muck and I will take them to the park, and pick up some flowers on the way."

"Good idea," said Bob.
"See you later, Wendy!"

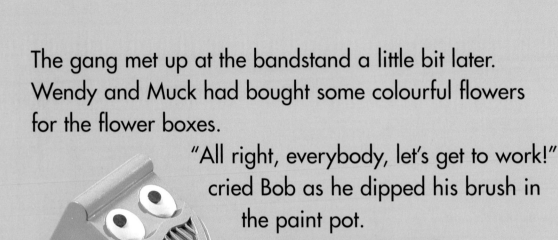

The gang met up at the bandstand a little bit later. Wendy and Muck had bought some colourful flowers for the flower boxes.

"All right, everybody, let's get to work!" cried Bob as he dipped his brush in the paint pot.

"**Can we fix it?**" asked Wendy.

"**Yes, we can!**" everyone shouted.

Rumble! Rumble! Rumble! went Roley as he flattened the ground with his rollers.

Click-Clack! Click-Clack! went Scoop as he opened and shut his front scoop.

Muck joined in with his shovel, **Bang! Bang! Bang!**

"You know, you lot make a pretty good band!" chuckled Bob as he and Wendy finished painting the bandstand.

Meanwhile poor Farmer Pickles still hadn't found his box of music.

"I'll just have to tell everybody that the concert's cancelled," he sighed.

He rang Bob to tell him the news. Bob was very disappointed. But then, he had a brilliant idea.

"Get over here as soon as you can, Farmer Pickles. I think I might be able to help!" he said looking at the team.

On his way to the park Farmer Pickles passed Spud.
"Are you going to play in the park?" Spud called.
"I don't think anybody's going to be playing in the park," said Farmer Pickles glumly.
Spud felt sorry for Farmer Pickles. "Oh well, you can play with one of my paper planes instead," he said.

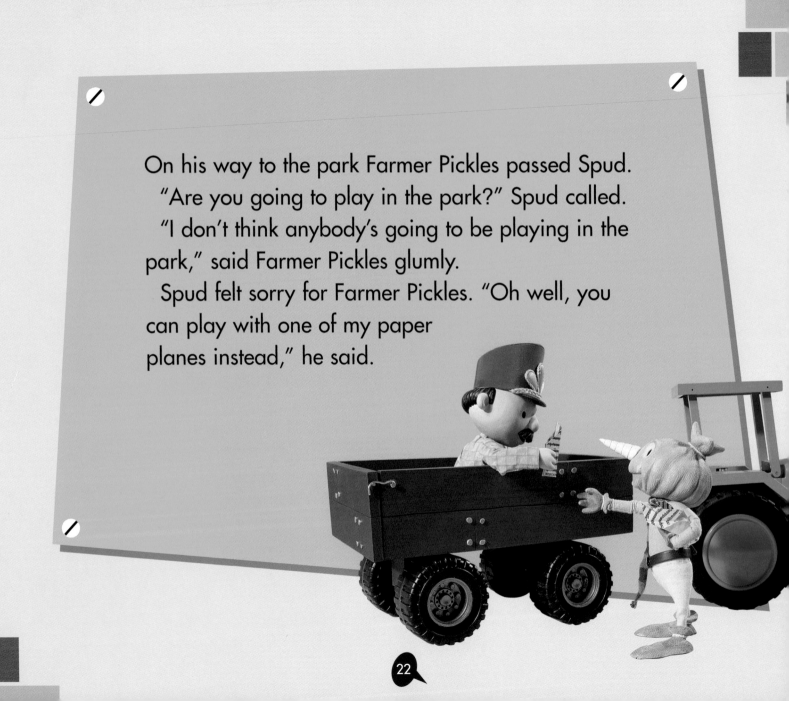

Farmer Pickles stared at the paper plane. "Spud, this is my music! Where did you get it from and where is it now?" he asked in amazement.

"I found it. I used it to scare off the crows. There's some in this field, and some in the top field," said Spud.

"Oh Spud, I think you'd better come with me," said Farmer Pickles. "You've got some explaining to do!"

When they got to the park Mr Bentley was standing by the new bandstand. "This looks splendid!" he said. "But… where's the band?"

"I'm sorry, they won't be able to play," Farmer Pickles told him. "We haven't got any music," he said looking sternly at Spud.

"Oww, I'm sorry, everyone. I found a box of paper that was great for making aeroplanes. I didn't know it was music," muttered Spud.

"Don't worry," said Bob quickly. "We've got a new band."

"A new band?" gasped Farmer Pickles.

"Yes, us!" said Bob as he waved towards the row of machines. **"We'll play!"**

"I'd love to be in a real band!" said Dizzy.

Farmer Pickles climbed onto the bandstand and waved his conductor's stick proudly.

"One, two, a-one, two, three, four!" he called.

Rumble! Rumble! Rumble! rolled Roley.

Clank! Clank! Clank! crashed Lofty.

Rattle! Rattle! Rattle!
giggled Dizzy.

Click-Clack! Click-Clack!
tapped Scoop.

Bang! Bang! Bang!
thumped Muck.

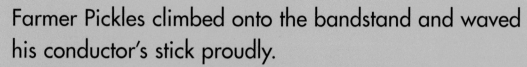

"Who needs an oom-pah-paah band when we've got Bob's Bandstand Rock and Rollers?" laughed Bob.

THE END!